I0526810

Written by: Mary Ann Wittman, Topeka, KS, mare30@cox.net

Illustrated by: Dan Pasley, Topeka, KS, dpgrafix187@yahoo.com

Published by: Jack Cobos Design, Topeka, KS, jackcobos@aol.com

Printed by: Josten's Printing & Publishing. Inc., Topeka, KS

Clemmie and the Mailman
A Story of Puppy Love!

By Mary Ann Wittman
Illustrated by Dan Pasley

Dedication

To our **USPS** Mail Carriers.
...and their furry, four-legged friends.

Neither snow, nor rain,
nor heat, nor gloom of night,

(nor dog,)

stays these couriers from their duty.

Some dogs don't like the mailman.

Some dogs are afraid of the mailman.

Some dogs want to bite the mailman.

But Clemmie is different. She LOVES her mailman.

She watches for the mailman every day from her pillow on the bed by the window.

She races to greet him on her walks. He returns her devotion with soft greetings and a tummy rub. Clemmie loves tummy rubs!

One day when Clemmie went out to play, she saw that the back gate was open. She wanted to explore the world outside of her fenced yard, so she crept through the opening.

This was very exciting! Clemmie did not have her leash on. She could run freely down the street!

First, she visited Ike and Mac, the basset hounds next door.
They liked to see Clemmie, and the hounds howled with happiness.

Then Clemmie ran across the street to see Toby,
who bounced with joy every time he saw her!
Clemmie was having fun! Doh-si-doh, around we go!

She left Toby to visit Charlie, the jumping beagle. Sometimes Charlie jumps so high that she jumps over her fence! Wow! Clemmie was enjoying herself.

Trotting on down the street, she noticed a big bush. Clemmie had a tiny little nose, but she was a very good sniffer. SOMETHING smelled interesting in that bush!

OH MY! It was Tigger, the big cat. Clemmie was curious about cats, so she padded close to him, hoping to be friends. But, Tigger did **NOT** want to be friends.

At last... Clemmie grew tired from all of her visiting, so she stretched out in the grass to rest. It was a hot day.

14

She was just falling asleep, when she heard a booming sound. Her ears perked up. What was that noise? The sky turned dark, and Clemmie felt a cool wind blow across her little face.

Rain sprinkled down into her fluffy fur. Now Clemmie was afraid. She wanted to go home! But, where WAS home? She did not know which way to run!

As the storm spread over the neighborhood, Clemmie huddled wet and cold under a big tree. She wished she had stayed in her nice, safe backyard.

Then she saw it! The big white mail truck!

And there was her mailman walking toward her through
the falling rain.

He bent down and softly called to her, "Clemmie, are you lost?" Frightened and soaked with rain, she crawled to him.

The mailman lifted her up and tucked her under his jacket.
She snuggled against him.

He gently placed her in the mail truck. "I'll take you home, girl," he promised. And he did.

Now Clemmie loves the mailman even more. And without her harness and leash, she never goes out the door!

The End

The CAST

Toby

Ike & Mac

Tigger

Charlie

Clemmie

The Artist

Dan

Dan has been a professional graphic artist for 10 years. He has produced over 15,000 art projects using a variety of media styles. This is the second children's book he has illustrated with Mary Ann. He lives in Topeka, Kansas.

The Author

Mary Ann

Mary Ann is an Adjunct Professor of Intensive English at Washburn University, and a freelance author. <u>Clemmie and the Mailman</u> is her third children's book, and the second in the *Dog Tales* series. She lives in Topeka, Kansas.